Tales under the Baobab Tree

—— Better Together ——

Cela and Ronnie Rootz

Tales Under The Baobab Tree
- Better Together -

1st Edition

Illustrator: George Nyiko Sky
Layout designer: Jessica Colley
Editor: Su-Mia Hoffmann

Prepared for print by Preflight Books, a division of BK Publishing (Pty) Ltd
www.preflightbooks.co.za

ISBN - 13
978-0-620-94283-6

For our miracle daughter Hannah Sahara.
Your radiant smile lights up the room.
Your willingness to share the Good News with others is a precious sight. Keep
on sharing His Word! Love you!

"...How beautiful are the feet of messengers who bring good news."
— Romans 10:15b

For the late David Hazzard, whose life challenged us to die living and not live to
die – and in the process spread the Good News!

"The path of the righteous is like the morning sun, shining ever brighter till the
full light of day."

— Proverbs 4:18

To children and families around the world.

Part of the royalties from the sale of this book will be donated to help children, families and communities in Southern Africa build sustainable initiatives and help realise their God-given potential.

The bolded words are in the Shona language of Zimbabwe.

"Oh wow!" Hannah exclaimed. She was amazed by all the different people sitting around the evening bonfire. The African sky was filled with bright stars and the smell of smoke hung in the air. Almost every race, colour, and culture was represented. It was exciting because this was her first bonfire in her new land.

It was a beautiful, warm night and the whole Roots family was sitting on **maponde** ('mats') under the enormous baobab tree, enjoying grilled maize cobs and roasted peanuts from the big bumper harvest.

"It was not always like this," grandfather Roots said. "Let me tell you a **ngano** ('tale')..."

"**Paivapo makare kare** ('Once upon a time, a long time ago'), in a land called **Mwene we Mutapa** ('King of the Land') there lived a beautiful biracial girl born of a **Kanata** (Canadian) mother and a Mwene we Mutapa father. Her name was **Sahara** ('dawn'). She lived with her parents **Runako** ('beautiful') and **Mhukahuru** ('big beast').

Sahara loved to smile and always carried her big smile and a very small hoe with her wherever she went. She loved to talk to people and encourage them in their time of distress. She also loved to join people in their time of laughter and joy."

Cela and Ronnie Rootz, also known as Cecelia and Felix Chiriseri, write for children and their families – to help them better understand what is going on in the world around them. They want children to learn that they can make a difference right where they are, no matter their age. Felix and Cecelia work in Southern Africa by walking alongside communities to help them find real long-term solutions to their challenges, while at the same time aiming to reduce the dependency mentality and show children and their families that they can lean on God as they realize their God-given potential.

Felix and Cecelia are blessed with a daughter, Hannah Sahara. They enjoy hiking, biking, camping and reading good books together.

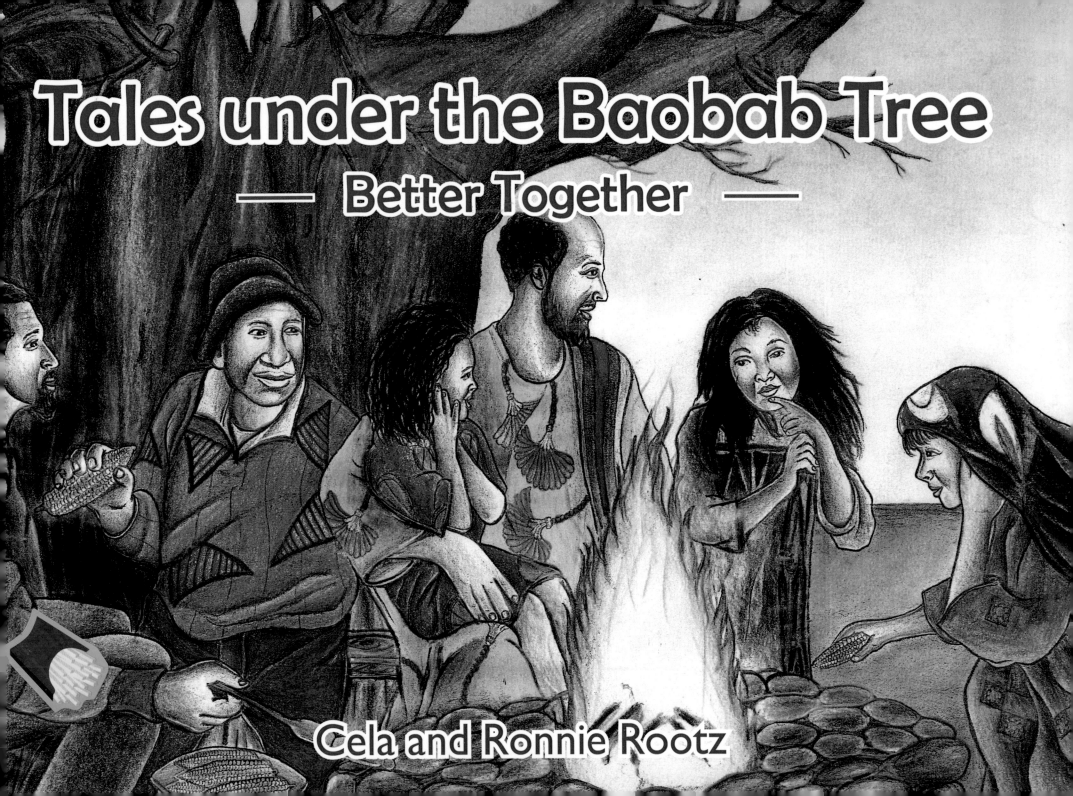